# Off the Bench

# Off the Bench

Written by Tom Mitchell

Illustrated by Amy Lane

**Collins**

# STEVE MASON
## ex-Sheffield Wednesday

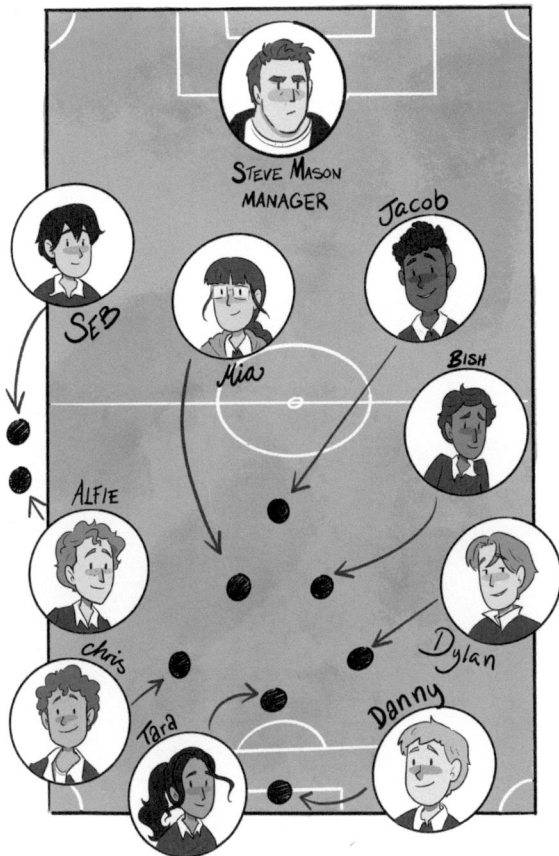

STEVE MASON MANAGER

Jacob

SEB

Mia

BISH

ALFIE

chris

Tara

Dylan

Danny

# MANAGER
## FULWOOD RANGERS U11

**Fulwood Rangers U11**

Goalkeeper: Danny Brown

Defender 1: Tara Patel

Defender 2: Chris Powell

Defender 3: Dylan Marr

Midfielder 1: Mia Smith

Midfielder 2: Bish Hussain

Striker 1: Jacob Callaghan

Sub 1: Seb Wilkins

Sub 2: Me, Alfie Saunders

Manager: Steve Mason (ex-Sheffield Wednesday)

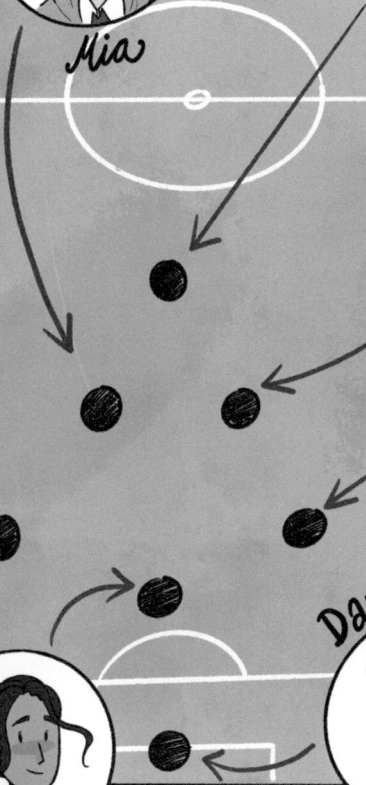

```
FPO
```

# 1 Inverted fullbacks

You probably think I'm good at football, but you'd be wrong. That's why I'm never picked. I *am* a brilliant manager, though. In ten years with the mighty Sheffield Wednesday on Football Manager, I've won the Premier League seven times, the Champions League three times, the FA Cup five times, the League Cup six times, and the Charity Shield once – but, you know, every manager has their weakness. Know this too – however good you think you are at EAFC (Xbox Ultimate Edition), I'll beat you. I'm not bragging, it's the truth. And, anyway, it's pretty much all I'm good at.

"And next on the line we have Alfie from Sheffield."

It was Mum's fault that I was about to speak on Radio 5 Live's 606, the football phone-in show. She'd had the programme on while she was cooking, and I'd made the mistake of mentioning that using inverted fullbacks (when the wide defender moves into a central midfield position) could sometimes leave Liverpool's defence exposed, and she'd been like, "You should ring in. Go on, Alfie, use my phone."

That's why Mum's phone was now on speaker in the middle of the kitchen table.

I didn't think they'd actually put me on. Neither did Dad, who's now watching, grinning and nodding. Sammy, my older brother, who either grunts or makes fun of me, definitely didn't. I'd made the mistake of catching his eye exactly when the producer had said I'd be on in 30 seconds, and I could tell that he was bursting to call me an idiot. Instead, he made do with kicking my ankles.

"Alfie! How's it going, mate?" Matt Weston, who'd played for England once, was actually talking to *me*. A ten-year-old who couldn't trap a ball if his life depended on it (according to my football coach). "You want to talk about Liverpool? Are you a fan?"

Sammy continued to kick my ankles. His eyes were dancing with joy, because he knew I was about to embarrass myself. Grinning, he nodded for me to speak.

"No," I said. "I support Sheffield Wednesday."

Sammy claimed to be Manchester City's

biggest fan, but he'd never once been to the Etihad Stadium (City's ground) and we lived in Sheffield. He bit his bottom lip, trying not to laugh out loud. Dad pointed a warning finger at him.

"Somebody has to," said Ricky Stone, ex-Leicester player, laughing. He was the show's co-host.

"Give over," said Weston.

"Sheffield Wednesday is the sixteenth most successful English football team. And they're currently the last team outside of the top division to win a major competition: the League Cup in 1991." The facts fell from me because I felt like I had to defend my team. That's why I'm a good manager. I know stuff.

"1991? How old are you, Alfie?" Sutton asked.

"Ten," I said, feeling my face glow with embarrassment. At least nobody from school would be listening.

"So what's this got to do with Liverpool?"

asked Weston. "Where are they in the list of successful teams?"

"In terms of combined competitions won, Liverpool is *the* most successful. But I was ringing to say that I think using two inverted fullbacks sometimes leaves their defence exposed."

Mum rubbed my back. Dad nodded. Even Sammy stopped kicking me for a moment. But despite how, at least to my family, I managed to sound like I knew what I was talking about, the ex-pros didn't engage. I could even hear Ricky Stone laugh. Again.

"Ten, did you say?" Weston said. "And do you play for a team? Because if you play football as well as you talk it, you'd be a superstar. Get Wednesday to sign you up!"

I cleared my throat. "Umm ... I'm part – "

Before I could explain that my team only played me if we were winning and it was the last five minutes (which hardly ever happened) *or* if literally nobody else was available (which did happen sometimes), Weston spoke.

"Thanks, Alfie. And now we've Euan on the line to talk about Brighton walking the ball into the net."

And as the researcher with the kind voice returned to tell me I'd done ever so well, I decided that the next time Mum suggested calling a national radio show, I'd say no. Or, at least, pretend that I was older.

**FPO**

# 2 Play to the whistle

My team, Fulwood Rangers, was in the U11 Sheffield Youth Cup's round of 16, which sounds impressive.

It's the stage before the quarter-finals but, to be honest, it was actually our first knock-out match because only 16 teams had entered.

Our coach, Steve, insisted we call him "gaffer" because that's what real footballers call their manager. And he should know because, believe it or not, he was once a professional footballer. He played for Sheffield Wednesday, which doesn't sound much but a) is, and b) they were actually in the Premier League once. Still, you'd not think he'd ever been a pro anything.

He wasn't much older than Dad but moved like he was underwater. Everything he did was in slow motion.

One thing that wasn't slow was our Thursday evening training sessions. There was loads of running, and never quickly enough for the gaffer. He always brought a foldable chair to the park, something the parents laughed about when he couldn't see them, and he'd shout "Faster, faster!" at us. Once Jacob, our star striker, asked him about tactics and he said, "What are they? A type of mint?"

And when we didn't react to the joke, he told us that football was a simple game made complicated by worrying about things like tactics. (We lost the game we played, after he'd said this, 4-0.)

Steve had thick hair the colour of gunmetal and a chin you could bend iron on. He was constantly chewing gum, but when Jacob did the same, Steve sent him to the benches. You'd think parents would complain about the way Steve did things, but the truth was that they didn't mind if it meant we were getting an hour's exercise on Thursday afternoons and more if there was a match on Sunday.

"Listen up, team," said Steve, as we huddled around him on the touchline. Because it was a match day, he was actually standing up. Past the tussocky pitch stood a line of parents, held back by a length of white tape. "Who can tell me how we're going to win this game?"

Tara, an old-style strong centre back, raised a hand. She always said what she thought, but knew better than to speak without permission.

"Yes, Tara."

"Stop them scoring goals," she said.

Steve scratched his intense chin.

"Aye," he said. "We don't want them scoring goals. But that's not what I had in mind. What about you, Mia?"

Mia wasn't one to speak. Her eyes expanded in horror. "Score more goals than the other team?" she mumbled.

Again, Steve scratched his chin.

"Yes, we want to be scoring more goals than the other team but, again, that's not what I was thinking. Come on, Alfie. I know you know, lad."

I did know. As did Tara. As did Mia. Because it was the same message every week, the same tactical instructions we were always given.

"Run ourselves into the ground, gaffer," I said.

"Exactly! Run ourselves into the ground! I didn't score the winner at Villa Park without running myself into the ground."

"Or we could start with a flat-back four?" I suggested.

Steve smiled, but didn't reply.

And so, the seven starters took their positions and I fist-bumped our goalkeeper Danny (good shot-stopper, not so great with his feet) because he said I was good luck. He also said my formation sounded better than running ourselves into the ground because he was the goalie, for one thing.

"Don't be afraid of diving!" I said to him. He narrowed his eyes in response, but anyone on the team will tell you that after he'd knocked his head against the post stretching for a save once, he'd always been a bit wary of diving.

I stood on the touchline alongside Steve, who was slowly putting another tab of gum into his mouth, and Seb who was recovering from a bike accident over the summer, which he claimed had left him with one leg longer than the other. His legs looked the same to me; even if they weren't, he could still play.

The referee, a frowning 17-year-old, blew his whistle and the match started. Almost immediately, we were under pressure. If I had to describe our formation, it wasn't the one I'd suggested – it was more of a flat-back seven. The whole team huddled near our goal like they were frightened of the opposition. Steve wasn't bothered with this, though; he didn't think it was too defensive.

Once, when a brave parent asked Steve whether he'd ever considered playing attacking football, Steve had asked whether that parent had ever played professionally. He also told them that, anyway, we didn't have the "flair players" to play the beautiful game.

Still, the opposition, New Star Wolves, didn't look like they had the players either. They must have taken about a dozen shots in the first 30-minute half, none of which were on target.

(We had no shots at all.)

At half-time, you might expect Steve to do a little tactical tinkering like, for instance, asking at least one of the team to cross the halfway line. But no.

"There's not enough running," he said. "You're giving them far too much time on the ball."

This was the basic theme of the half-time talk, although he spent a good five minutes saying the same thing but using different words.

I raised my hand.

"Yes, Alfie?"

"How about we go 2-1-2-1 and Mia and Bish could support Jacob in attacking positions, gaffer?"

"Umm," said Bish, our midfielder, trembling a little. "I'm not sure I'm good at attacking."

But Steve wasn't interested in my suggestion. He didn't need to ask if I'd ever played professional football. Instead, he raised a single eyebrow and said, "Let's get at them, second half!"

Not long after the whistle had blown, Dylan got injured. He pulled a muscle in a 50/50 challenge and limped off the pitch.

Steve looked at me, then he looked at Seb. "Think you can manage, Seb?" he asked.

"I'm finding it hard to walk, gaffer, let alone run. Why not put Alfie on?"

Steve slapped him on the back. "Let's not question the manager's decisions, eh? I'm sure you'll be fine. Do you remember the game against Power Athletic? How many own goals was it, Alfie, son?"

"Three," I said. "But two were deflections."

Seb reluctantly got up and joined the others on the pitch.

Amazingly, we won the game 1-0. Not because of our ability, or Steve's tactical tweaks, but because of a dog. It was coming up to the last five minutes of the second half and New Star Wolves had just taken what felt like their fiftieth shot. It ballooned over the bar, and the watching spectators groaned.

As Danny went to take our goal kick, a black greyhound ran onto the pitch, appearing from nowhere as if it was from another dimension. Although no great passer, Danny could welly the ball impressively and as it spooned up into the air, the dog sniffed about the centre circle. It didn't look much of a football fan.

"Dog!" shouted New Star Wolves' central midfielder, pointing at the dog. He wasn't the only member of his team to focus on the woofy intruder instead of the game. But the referee, although raising his neon orange whistle to his lips, hadn't blown.

"Make yourself useful, son," said Steve, pushing me forwards.

I stumbled onto the pitch, not knowing how I might catch the dog. Dad has terrible allergies, so we've never had a pet of any kind. I crept up on the greyhound, and attempted to tackle it from behind.

The ball bounced nearby. It was a high bounce and it spun off into the opponent's half. The dog chased after it but stopped in the centre circle. Without turning, the greyhound sensed it was

being stalked, so stopped its sniffing and darted off towards the spectators, ducking away through someone's legs. I didn't think I could follow – every hunter has their limits – so I stopped at the touchline and turned to watch the game.

The bounce of the ball, and the distraction of the dog, took out the entire visiting defence. Jacob controlled the ball and found himself one-on-one with the keeper. The opposition coach shouted for the keeper to come out and, as Jacob entered the box, he did. Jacob took a shot. It hit the keeper's knee and spun off to the side. We watched in silence as it bounced once, hit the left-hand post, and dribbled into the net.

Our supporters cheered as the team ran to congratulate Jacob, who stood there with the sun hitting his blond hair perfectly. Well, all except Seb, who was clearly fake-limping.

"Get in! What did I tell you?" called Steve, pointing at the opposition coach.

"There was a dog on the pitch!" replied the coach, turning from Steve to shout at the referee. "There was a dog on the pitch!"

An adult from the visiting side shouted too. "You can't be allowing dogs on football fields," he said. "Disallow the goal."

But there was no Video Assistant Referee. The ref had clearly seen the dog but still awarded the goal to us. Unbelievable!

When the final whistle blew, we were in the quarter-finals.

FPO

# 3 Smash and grab

Two weeks later …

"Do you think you might get some game time today?" asked Dad, as we walked to the playing fields.

"Sometimes Steve forgets that *everyone* should get a chance to play," said Mum. "No matter how – " She paused to try to find the right word. She failed.

"… developed their talents," said Dad.

I didn't need reminding that I was more three-games-a-season defender than 30-goal-a-season-striker. And Dad probably saw that on my face. "I mean, you won the last game, Alfie. If you hadn't run onto the pitch to get that dog, Jacob would never have scored."

"Hmm," I said, because sometimes, when you're talking to your parents, making a noise is better than risking words.

Every Sunday morning, the fields were a kaleidoscope of colour and today was no different. Fulwood wore all-red, which I didn't much like because that was the colour of Sheffield United's stripes. The visiting sides wore their away kits – the teams could be playing opponents from the city or surrounding Yorkshire. And then there were the spectators with their less-brightly coloured loungewear, and the younger brothers and sisters of the players, who ran about in the stark white of Real Madrid or the pale blue of Man City.

It was a busy scene and not just in colour. There was shouting too: "man on" and "leave it" and names called for passes. There were coaches complaining and referees blowing whistles and parents shouting encouragement. And then there were the smells from the clubhouse, the toast and eggs and beans that wafted across the fields.

If you weren't hungry when the match started, you were by the end.

Our corner of the playing fields was next to the entrance closest to home; the gap in the hedgerow that had a sign next to it saying: "Not an official entrance. The club accepts no responsibility for injuries suffered when entering here." And as we stepped onto the grass, which would soon be mud, Dad, not always the most observant of people, immediately saw the problem.

"Doesn't look like the other team are here, then," he said. "Steve won't be happy."

I jogged onto the pitch where Mia, Chris and Danny were trying to hit the crossbar from the edge of the area. Steve stood nearby, but with his back turned to the team. He had a phone to his ear.

Tara saw me coming and knocked a ball into my path. It hit a divot as I lifted my foot to control it. Making like I was expecting this, I struck a clean half volley. This sounds good but what actually happened was that I whacked the ball as hard as I

could and it missed the goal by a mile, zooming off closer to the corner flag and whistling past the ear of a spectator in a puffer jacket, who turned and waved his fist. He had a *very* purple face.

Steve was off the phone and waved us over.

"Huddle up!" he commanded.

We stood in a tight horseshoe shape around the coach. I was expecting the same old team talk – the familiar instruction to run around a lot and to never stop running. Instead, the gaffer announced something surprising.

"I've just been on the phone with the manager of the Crosspool Crusaders." He eyed us up and scratched his chin. He was milking the moment for maximum drama. "And he told me that his minibus has broken down and they'll likely be late. Now, you know that there's one thing that I can't abide." We all nodded. "Alfie? What's that?"

I cleared my throat. "Not giving 110%, gaffer," I said.

"Aye. Not giving 110%. I'm not going to say you're wrong. But there's something else too. Anyone?"

Bish raised a shaking hand. "Umm ... being late?" he asked.

"Yes!" bellowed Steve, which made everyone

jump. "Being late! So when the manager of Crosspool Crusaders, who's never played the game at any level, offered me the choice of postponing the match or accepting a bye, I naturally took the bye."

Steve's eyebrows arched as he awaited our reaction. The only thing is we didn't really react. And for good reason too.

"So what's a bye?" asked Dylan.

Steve shook his head. "Unbelievable," he said. "It's a win without playing. We don't have to play. They've forfeited the quarter-final. Fulwood Rangers, we're in the semis!"

There was a brief pause before Tara spoke. "For real, gaffer?" she said.

Steve closed his eyes and took a deep breath. "Do I strike you as the kind of man to joke about these things?"

"No," said Tara. "You don't."

"Wait a minute," said Mia. We all turned to her, even Steve. "We're in the semis, people!"

This was the loudest I'd ever heard her speak.

Fulwood Rangers U11s roared approval, and we all bounced up and down, like teams do when they've won trophies. Even I got involved. And Seb too, even though he said his leg hurt.

"Don't get too excited yet," said Steve. "It's a huge disappointment to crash out in the semis. England 1990. And 1996."

"If we haven't got a game, what are we going to do?" asked Jacob, looking across to the spectators. They were standing at the touchline, unaware we'd already won.

"What do you think?" asked Steve.

We all knew the answer, but I felt that I needed to try at least. "How about practising a 1-1-3-1 formation attack?"

This wasn't the right answer. The right answer was ...

... running practice.

FPO

# 4 Tapped up

On Tuesday, there was a knock at our front door. No, Dad hadn't ordered another curry and, strangely, it was for me.

"Alfie! You've friends calling," Mum shouted up the stairs.

I came downstairs from some particularly boring SATs practice to see Jacob and Tara standing at my front door; this was doubly strange because I didn't even think they were friends outside of football.

"After school tomorrow," said Tara.

"High street coffee shop," added Jacob, smiling.

And then, without even saying goodbye, they turned and left.

After school the next day, I told Mum that I was going to meet some friends. Ten minutes later, I was in the coffee shop with the rest of the team. This wasn't our first visit; sometimes we'd go after matches. There was a booth in the back corner, and we all squeezed in. Some of us bought drinks, so the servers would let us stay as long as we wanted.

"Steel City Stars," announced Jacob. "That's who we're playing in the semis. And we were thinking it'd be good to talk about the game, you know, away from Steve."

"Sick," said Dylan.

Tara frowned at him. "What do you mean *sick*? Do you know the Steel City Stars?"

Dylan cleared his throat, his coolness fading a degree. "No," he said.

The Steel City Stars were the envy of every

youth side in South Yorkshire. John Whitgift, the owner, had poured money into the club. They had their own hybrid grass training pitch that was *inside* a building; it was part of a training complex with a swimming pool and a gym. People said it was better than Wednesday's own training ground. There were rumours that their players were given gifts like games consoles or phones when they signed up. Their kit was all black; if you were a primary school footballer and you thought you were better than everyone else, you'd play for Steel City Stars.

There was one strange thing about the team, though. For all their money, they'd never won a single trophy. They were a kind of opposite of Man City. Kind of.

"Could someone buy me a chocolate muffin?" asked Chris, but before anyone answered, Bish pointed to the counter across the café. "Look! No way!" he whispered. "It's Steve. We're in so much trouble if he finds out we're having a secret team meeting!"

"I knew I shouldn't have come," said Dylan.

"Quiet!" commanded Tara, craning her neck. "Who's he with? I can't see."

Although we ducked and dived like gophers, Steve's friend had his back turned to us. From this angle, it looked like he was wearing a suit, not the usual sportswear our coach wore. They made their order and waited at the end of the counter for their drinks.

"I'll go," gulped Mia, speaking like she was volunteering for a dangerous mission behind enemy lines.

"What?" asked Tara.

"I said I'll go."

As she left the booth, Dylan whispered, "Don't get caught!"

Between the seating area and the counter, there was a stout condiment station, the size of a couple of chests of drawers put together lengthways. Ignoring the older couple sitting at the table right next to this, Mia hid herself behind the furniture. Steve and the stranger were sitting on the other side.

I felt like my heart might explode. It wasn't that Mia was in danger; *we* were more likely to

get seen. All Steve needed to do was turn around.

"If you've got a phone, get it out. If you've a hoodie, put it up," I said.

Adults tend not to notice kids if they're acting how they think kids act. My tactic worked.

Eventually, Steve and his friend left, the doorbell sounding as they exited. We were safe!

Mia darted out from behind the condiments and back to the booth. I've never seen her move so quickly, not on the football field at least. "The man!" she said. "I know him!"

We waited, but she didn't continue.

"And?" said Seb. We all leant in to hear what she was saying.

"It's John Whitgift."

Everyone looked at each other with raised eyebrows; there was no other way to react really.

"Who's John Whitgift?" asked Dylan.

"John Whitgift? Only the owner of Steel City Stars," said Jacob.

"No way," said Dylan.

"Way," said Tara.

"And that's not all," Mia continued. "Steve had a hot chocolate with extra marshmallows. And John Whitgift paid for the drinks and said, 'It's not like Fulwood will win anyway'."

"I never took him for a hot chocolate drinker," said Bish.

"I don't think the hot chocolate is the important point here," Tara said.

"What did Mr Whitgift mean?" Chris asked.

Tara looked at Jacob and Jacob looked at Tara.

"We're playing them. In the semis. We're

playing Steel City Stars," Jacob said.

"Well, he's right then. There's no way we're going to beat them. Their striker had a trial at Leeds."

Tara put her head in her hands, before raising her head and speaking. "Don't you get it? They're fixing the match. Steve was obviously agreeing to lose on purpose. Whitgift must think we're in with a chance if he's meeting with Steve. We've been betrayed, people. They've fixed the match."

I spoke up. I had to say something. "No way," I said. "Mia probably misheard. No offence, Mia. I mean, Steve can be mean and angry and makes us run lots and won't shut up about being a professional footballer, even though he only played for Wednesday four times, but he wants to win too. He'd never do that."

"Wouldn't he?" asked Bish.

"I know what I heard," said Mia, quietly.

No one felt like talking tactics after that. Dylan suggested we go to the park for a kick-about but nobody had brought a ball. Before I left, I asked Jacob what he thought we should do.

He shrugged. "What can we do?" he said. "It's not as if anyone's brave enough to talk to Steve about it. And Steve doesn't listen to anything our parents say anyway."

"How do you know?" I asked.

"Mum asked him why we weren't practising passing," Jacob told me. "Steve told her he was the ex-pro, and running round the pitch was good for us."

When I arrived back home, Dad was cooking dinner (putting frozen pizzas in the oven) and Mum was telling Sammy off for getting another lunchtime detention. I thought I'd be able to sneak to my room without being stopped, I had a lot of thinking to do, but I was wrong. Mum called to me as I took my first step onto the stairs.

"I hope you've taken your trainers off," she said. I looked down to my feet. I hadn't. I turned to inspect the hallway's carpet. There was a trail of dark footprints, which was weird because I'd definitely not stepped in any mud. "Sad news about your coach," she called out. "He does get you lot running about. I've always been impressed."

I forgot about the mud. "What?" I shouted. "What about him?"

"He messaged the group chat. After the school holidays, he'll be joining another club. He says they made him an offer he couldn't refuse."

"What other club?" I asked.

"That rich one. Steel City Stars."

Upstairs, I lay on my bed. I knew exactly what

had happened. John Whitgift saw a chance of winning. In return for throwing the game, he'd obviously offered Steve a job. And Steve had accepted.

We *had* been betrayed. And by an ex-Wednesday player too. It doesn't get much worse than that.

**FPO**

# 5 Running laps

Even by Steve's standards, Thursday's training had a lot of running. In fact, there was nothing *but* running. Normally, there'd be some skill activities and then we'd split into a small game. Not this time. It was exhausting.

We did laps of the pitch, and Steve sat in his collapsible chair and looked at his phone. He occasionally lifted his head to shout at us to keep running. Some parents came to training and watched from the same touchline that they stood along during the Sunday games. Dad accused Mum of treating it as a social event, of doing nothing but catching up with friends. Mum always replied that there were better places to do this than

damp playing fields in the Sheffield suburbs.

After our fourth lap, the parents had stopped chatting. As we passed them the fifth time, Mum asked whether this was all we were going to do. I was too tired to speak, so did a kind of awkward shrug as I passed.

When we reached Steve's chair on the eighth lap, he called for us to stop. The team bent over, hands on knees, panting wildly. Bish looked like he might die, which, fortunately, he didn't. I was too tired to even talk tactics.

"See?" asked Steve. "None of you are fit enough. It's all that screen time." He returned to his phone, as he waited for us to catch our breath. "Now, I've a few things to say."

I noticed Jacob look to Tara. She raised her eyebrows, but they were about to be disappointed. Steve didn't mention the Steel City Stars at all. He didn't say much about anything, to be honest.

He lined us up on the touchline and spoke from his chair. This was unusual. Even Steve, who claimed standing for any length of time was dangerous, due to an old knee injury, would normally get up to deliver his Thursday training talk. I could smell mud and grass; it might almost have been a normal afternoon.

"Don't worry about Sunday," he said. "They'll beat us and they'll beat us easily. Just enjoy yourselves. And so there are no surprises on the day, I want you all to know that I'll be mixing the team up a bit. We can't be relying on stray dogs or broken-down coaches every week. Have we ever heard of total football? Ajax? Johan Cruyff? Alfie?"

I nodded. "It's when any outfield player can take the role of any other outfield player, gaffer."

"Aye," said Steve. "Exactly. Good job." At this, he stood and folded up his chair. "Anyway, see you all on Sunday."

"Umm ... is total football a great idea, gaffer?" I asked. "We don't have Cruyff on the team."

"We don't need him. Not when we've got Jacob, eh lad? Get yourselves rested and I'll see you when I see you."

Seb made the mistake of looking at his watch.

"I'm well aware, young man, that we're finishing early this week. But do you know how much I get paid to train you lot? Zero. That's what. And I should also get compensation for watching you lose almost every week too. Any problems with any of that?"

Everyone looked to their feet. Normally, he'd

tell us to eat a banana and get a good night's sleep before the match. His phone rang, and he looked at the number and said, "I've got to take this." He lifted his chair over his shoulder and walked away.

As the team drifted over to our parents, Jacob called for me to stop. "It's exactly what we thought!" he said. "Steve's going to make us lose."

"We'll lose anyway," said Bish, quietly.

"He's going to swap our positions around," I said. "Total football."

"We all know you're a legend at Football Manager, Alfie. Didn't you win the Champions League with Wednesday?" asked Tara.

"Three times," I said, but I wasn't bragging.

"And my dad says you were on the radio and made more sense than Ricky Stone," said Dylan.

"Doesn't take much," said Danny.

I hadn't realised anyone had heard me. I could

feel my cheeks glowing in embarrassment.

"You could manage us, Alfie!" said Chris. Mia nodded in agreement. "You're always talking tactics and formations. Also, does anyone have any shin pads? I've lost mine."

Tara rolled her eyes.

"I can't," I said, keeping my voice low so our parents couldn't hear. "Until he leaves, Steve's the boss. And I'm just a kid. Imagine how purple his face would get if I started coaching from the sidelines. And, also, I don't have any shin pads spare."

I had a strange feeling in my chest. I didn't want to say any more in case it got worse. Fine, I knew a bit about tactics, enough to realise that "total football" would be a total disaster, but I couldn't defy Steve. He was our manager.

"It doesn't matter about Steve," said Tara. "He's abandoned us."

I spotted Mum with her bobble hat and coffee flask and started to jog towards her.

"It's the semi-final. We've a chance of getting through. Steel City aren't as good as they think they are. And the final is at Hillsborough," Tara called after me.

I stopped jogging and turned to face her. "What?"

"You're a Wednesday fan. Wouldn't you love to play at their stadium?" asked Bish. "But, like, it's fine if we don't. Ignore me."

"I'd never get on the pitch," I shrugged.

"Please, Alfie!" called Mia. "We're begging you."

I waved them away. I was pro at Football Manager but that didn't mean I could lead an actual team. And anyway, what was that quote Dad always repeated, from manager Brian Clough? "Football is a simple game made complicated by idiots." Brian won the European Cup *twice* with Nottingham Forest, so he would know.

Steve had set us up but whatever his instructions, I'm sure the team could manage. Like always, we'd need to score goals and avoid conceding them. That hadn't changed. And I'd sit on the bench, as usual.

But as we were walking home, I couldn't ignore the feeling that I was letting the team down.

```
FPO
```

# 6 A game of two halves

"Look at them," said Bish, with the kind of hushed awe you might expect if we were sharing a pitch with Barcelona.

"Yeah. Their strip is sick," added Dylan.

And it was. All black with their yellow club badge and Whitgift Solutions, the sponsor, written across their chests in yellow too. The team went through their individual warm-up exercises, looking worryingly like they knew what they were doing.

"Check out number 7," said Tara, pointing out a boy who was juggling the ball on the instep of his right foot.

As we watched, he lobbed the ball up and then struck it on a full volley. The ball arrowed into the top corner from about 18 metres. If Jacob had even attempted a similar shot, we'd have all cheered and clapped and whooped. Steel City Stars weren't bothered.

As they warmed up in their goalmouth, we did the same at the opposite end of the pitch.

Steve was running a training exercise that we sometimes practised. You start midway in the half, and you pass the ball out to Steve. He knocks the ball back and you have two touches to score. This morning, Steve was hitting the ball back harder than usual, which made it difficult to control. Normally, he'd lose his temper if the ball went spinning off in the wrong direction but, today, he was unusually quiet. It was like someone had turned the volume down. When he passed the ball to me, it hit my knee and shot up in the air. I tried to strike the ball as it descended, and I did, but it sliced away off to the left.

"Nice effort," called Steve. It was like I'd woken up in an opposite world, where Steve was always nice. "Keep your eye on the ball."

The referee came over to let Steve know it was five minutes to kick-off. Today, because it was the semi-final maybe, the official was an adult with very large eyebrows and a stern expression.

"Right, everyone huddle," called Steve. We formed our familiar horseshoe around him. "As

I said on Thursday, we're going to mix things up a bit today. It's total football, attacking style! Danny, you're in goal. Mia, Bish, Dylan, you're defence. In midfield, we'll have Seb and Chris. And upfront – "

We'd almost stopped listening. Sure, the mixing up of midfield and defence was alarming, as was the inclusion of Seb, who still claimed one of his legs was longer than the other. But we never expected what would happen next.

"... Tara."

"What?" said Tara. "I can't play striker."

"Sure you can," replied Steve. "Just make sure you run around and give the ball some welly."

I looked at Jacob. If I didn't know any better, I'd have thought he might start crying.

"Gaffer?" asked Dylan, looking to Jacob as he spoke. "Do you want us to lose?"

"Don't be daft. How did you ever get that idea? Danny's still our keeper, right?"

"Because you've dropped our best player. And Tara's never scored a single goal ever. She's a defender."

At that very moment, I saw Steve looking over at the Steel City Stars owner, John Whitgift, who was standing with the opposition spectators. He had a very orange tan and wore sunglasses, despite the day being overcast. He was also giving Steve a knowing smile. You might think this would have caused our coach some embarrassment. But you don't know Steve. He smiled right back.

"Right," said Steve. "Hands up, who's ever played professionally." He made a play of inspecting the team, waiting for a hand. "Thought not. How about we do what our coach tells us and stop moaning. Jacob, lad, you'll get on later. And you might even score us a goal. Wanting to lose! The very thought. I mean, it's not like I've put Alfie in the team. No offence, Alfie."

I cleared my throat but couldn't think of anything smart to say because, actually, I was a bit offended.

Steel City Stars got a penalty in the first minute. I'd like to claim that it was a dodgy decision, but it wasn't. Bish, who was about as good at tackling as a bowl of ice cream, stuck out a leg as their number 7 ran past, dribbling the ball, causing the Steel City player to fall to the ground.

The referee pointed to the spot and blew his whistle. Nobody complained, not even Steve, which was a first.

The number 7 high-fived every member of their team, which was, like, *the* most annoying thing I'd ever seen. Still, I'd seen Danny save penalties before. Maybe he'd dive this time?

We stood around the penalty box. Their player placed the ball on the penalty spot, counted four steps back and waited. The referee blew the whistle. The number 7 jogged towards the ball and, with predictable arrogance, attempted a Panenka. This, if you didn't know, is when the penalty-taker lightly chips the ball down the middle, hoping to trick the goalkeeper into diving to the left or right. And maybe if the Steel City Stars player had known about Danny's lack of diving, he wouldn't have tried it. Because, as it turned out, Danny just stood there, and the ball slowly looped towards him and he caught it.

On the touchline, I turned to Jacob and we high-fived each other. Ironically. I was so excited I almost hugged Steve but he was standing further away and had a weird kind of non-smile plastered above his big chin. Also, he wasn't a hugger.

I lost count of how many shots there were in the first half. And, obviously, they were all theirs. Tara ended up playing more like an extra defender, and the game was like one of those you see on TV when Liverpool play Bromley in the FA Cup, and the lower league team is pinned in their own box, knocking the ball away however they can manage and having no ambition but to keep the score down.

There was one amazing moment when a through-ball managed to beat our line of defenders who, for once, weren't in the six-yard box. And with their striker one-on-one with the keeper, Dylan somehow caught up and got a toe to the ball, just as the number 7 was drawing back a foot to fire. Even Steve couldn't help himself and applauded. I could imagine Gary Neville praising Dylan on TV.

The highlights would also feature their fourth free kick; the one given after Seb had pulled back a player by their shirt because they'd run past him,

and he could only walk. The whistle sounded, and
the opposition's midfielder took a shot from 23
metres out. This time, Danny dived, stretching
an arm to the top corner of the net.

He didn't save the goal with his hand, though. Somehow, if you can believe it, the ball hit the top of his head, bounced against the underside of the bar, and then off back into play. The Steel City players were so surprised they didn't react in time and Mia managed to clear.

The first half finished 0-0 and, yes, we'd not been in their half at all, and we'd not had a single shot. In any other circumstance (like playing in a match our coach wasn't actively trying to lose), we might have gone into the break thinking we had a chance. All it took was a single moment, a mistake from their defence. That's the beauty of football: sometimes the best team doesn't win.

Steve cleared his throat as we huddled around him. "This is a cup match. And it's a cup match we're lucky not to be losing. There's lots of the season left, with loads of league matches. That's why they schedule the cup so early, to get it out of the way. What I'm trying to say is there's no point tiring ourselves out today, exhausting our bodies when we've a run of league matches coming up, games we might win."

Was Steve *actually* telling us *not* to run ourselves into the ground? Was he really instructing us to lower the pace? If ever I'd had any doubts about him wanting us to lose, they'd now been destroyed.

"Why don't we just keep it simple? Try to control possession with short passing, gaffer?" I suggested.

"Let's keep the coaching to the coach, please," said Steve, with less anger than you might imagine.

"But you're leaving," said Tara, spitting out the words angrily. "What do you care about the team? About the league."

Bish actually gasped. We'd never heard anyone talk to Steve like this before. The gaffer didn't explode, though. He even gave us a weird grin.

"Ask any pro, they want their current team to win, regardless of whether they're leaving or not."

"You're joining them. We know," said Jacob, nodding over at the Steel City team.

"Aye," nodded Steve. "What of it? Are we back on this silly me-wanting-to-lose thing again? How about we talk about the game? Did I tell the team to take no shots? I don't think I did."

Things must have been serious because Steve hadn't lost his temper. In fact, he was treating the whole thing like it was a laugh.

Seb raised his hand. "Can I come off, please, gaffer? My leg's well hurting."

"Come off? Come off? In all my years, I've never had a player wanting to be substituted. And you lot are claiming *I* don't want to win! All right, have it your own way. Danny, you swap places with Seb. Seb, you're in goal. You won't have to worry about your legs there."

"But I've never played in goal before," said Seb.

"It's fine. It's like playing outfield but you can use your hands. And Danny, my boy, remember you can't use your hands now you're in midfield.

Sorted. Oh, and see if you can manage a shot in the second half, everyone. That'd be grand." He nodded, waiting for a reaction. "All right?" A few of us murmured a response. "I can't hear you!"

Like a Year 2 class all saying "good morning" to their teacher, we spoke in chorus. "Yes, gaffer."

"Anyway, I've got to run to the bathroom," Steve said. "See you in a bit." And he set off towards the clubhouse at his usual steady pace.

"You've got to do something, Alfie," said Chris.

The team nodded like a gang of gophers.

"Why me?" I asked.

"There's a phrase for this," said Danny, looking to the sky for inspiration. "My dad uses it. 'Transferable skills', that's what. You're a pro manager on the computer and you can be a pro manager for us."

I felt like I had the weight of the ocean on me.

I could talk tactics, but nobody usually listened. Still, it seemed like I didn't have an option.

"OK, OK," I said. "I'll talk to Steve."

Muted cheers rose from the team as Seb pointed at his watch. "You've got five minutes before the second half kicks off."

FPO

# 7 Locker room banter

As I crossed the pitch and headed for the clubhouse, I'd never felt so nervous. I'd also never felt my parents' eyes burning so intensely into the side of my head as I passed their side of the pitch and didn't stop walking.

I knew, despite Steve's less than usual amount of anger, that there was nothing I could say to change his behaviour. For one thing, he'd ask me if I'd ever played professional football. Guaranteed. For another thing, a question gnawing at my insides: what was it that I was trying to do?

"Please set up the team and inspire them so they have at least a chance of scoring a goal?"

I could ask that.

By the time I reached the clubhouse, I'd decided to limit my request to having Jacob play upfront. He was our best player, he scored goals. But as I waited outside the toilets, I wondered whether I could do something without having to talk to Steve at all, and he'd never know it was me …

If the long pole, one of those you spike into the ground to make a temporary goal, hadn't been leaning close by, I might never have done it. But it was, and I did.

I picked up the pole and threaded it through the silver C-shaped handle on the toilet door. The pole passed either side of the doorframe, meaning that the door couldn't be opened from inside. Steve must have heard my banging about, as he almost immediately tried the door. The pole bent slightly but didn't give. He thumped away at the other side.

"Open this door! Now!" he shouted.

I tiptoed away, and told myself not to feel too guilty; someone was bound to need the toilet at some

point and they could let the gaffer out.

Emerging into the fresh air, I jogged past other games in play and back to our familiar corner. I didn't need much time to change what was needed, but before I reached the team to explain my plan, the referee stopped me. The others looked over apprehensively from the touchline; the Steel City Stars players were in position, waiting to kick off.

"Where's your coach?" the referee asked.

It was time to lie and make a total commitment to

the plan. "He's not feeling well. He said I should manage the team until he gets back."

"You?" asked the referee, his eyebrows lowering. "How old are you?"

"Come on! What's taking you so long?" It was John Whitgift shouting.

The referee raised a hand to acknowledge his complaint. "Fine, fine," he said. "You've one minute to sort your players out and then we're restarting whether they're on the pitch or not."

I ran across to the team. They waited for me in silence, like a class expecting a visit from the head teacher.

"OK. Let's go back to how things should be. Danny, you're in goal. Tara, Chris, Dylan: defence. Mia, Bish: midfield. And Jacob, you're upfront. Look, this lot like to really push forward to put us under pressure, so as soon as you get the ball, knock it long. Jacob, don't worry about defending, stand on the halfway line and wait for our clearances. Is that OK, everyone?"

They all nodded.

"Where's Steve?" asked Bish, shaking a little.

"He's my problem," I replied.

"Sure, that sounds cool," said Dylan. "But where is he actually?"

"I locked him in the clubhouse toilet."

Half the team gasped; the other half nervously laughed. I was saved from explaining myself by the referee blowing his whistle and waving for us to take to the pitch.

"Good luck, everyone!" I said, as they jogged away from Seb and me.

"Do you think we've got a chance, gaffer?" Seb asked.

"Maybe not a massive one. But better than before. As long as Steve doesn't escape too soon."

FPO

# 8 Good and bad

Something had changed, and it was obvious what. We took kick-off, and as soon as Jacob passed the ball to Chris, one of their midfielders ploughed into the back of him. Jacob was knocked to the ground and let out a little scream. The referee stopped play and talked to the midfielder. He wasn't shown a yellow, though, even though it was possibly a red-card challenge.

Clearly, they'd been told to play rough. Any 50/50 ball and the Steel City players were full in, elbows and knees and showing their studs. They gave away free kicks, all of which we wasted, but were never aggressive enough to get into more trouble. They'd obviously been well coached.

But, in all fairness, it didn't help their game. Maybe our players going back to their usual positions made the difference, but there was no longer any rhythm to the oppositions' play. And, yes, it still felt like it was only a matter of time before they scored, but after 15 minutes, the score remained 0-0 and we'd even had a couple of chances.

I don't like to big myself up, and anyone watching might have given the same advice, but twice Jacob was played through from a long ball. Once a defender got back and made him snatch his shot, which their keeper easily saved. The second time, Jacob being Jacob, tried to do something spectacular and smashed the ball from way out when he could easily have dribbled forwards more. At full stretch, the keeper palmed the ball over. It was a decent effort, to be fair, but could have been so much more.

And then came their goal.

There was a quick one-two in the midfield that bypassed Mia and Bish with ease. Suddenly four of their players, spread across the pitch, were

bearing down on our three defenders; no one knew whether to challenge or hold their ground.

"Push up!" I called. "And get some tackles in!"

But it was too late. As Chris passed the ball to Dylan a Steel City player barged through and intercepted it. Tara tried her best to get across to challenge him for the ball, but it was no good. He was one-on-one with Danny, who made a huge effort to look big, to narrow the angles, but the attacker didn't hesitate. It was one of those moments when you knew the ball would hit the back of the net before it actually did.

Danny spread out as the ball was struck in an arc. He managed to get a touch, but not enough. The ball nestled into the corner of the goal, and the net rustled tragically. As the Steel City Stars ran towards their goal-scorer as if he'd just won them the World Cup, I asked Seb how much longer was left.

"Seven minutes," he said.

I looked past the celebrations, towards the clubhouse. There was no sign of Steve. I knew exactly what he'd say on returning, if we lost. He'd claim we'd have had a chance with him, that whoever locked him in the toilets had cost the team. Would I admit it was me?

"Wait," said Seb. "What's going on?"

I turned my focus back to the pitch. Steel City were no longer celebrating. Instead, they were surrounding the referee, who was very clearly making a pushing gesture that meant ...

... a foul!

"No way!" I said.

"Sick!" said Seb.

"Keep going!" I called to the team.

"That's easy for you to say!" shouted Tara; her face was shining with exhaustion.

Play restarted. From the free kick, Danny knocked the ball long, as instructed. And, for once, he managed a solid connection. It bounced on the halfway line and arced high. Jacob was on the shoulder of the last defender and predicted what might happen. The ball curled into their half and Jacob was away with it.

My heart caught in my throat. Could it be happening? Might we actually score?

And then a defender, making up ground to catch our star striker, dived in with both feet, scraping his studs along the back of Jacob's calves. You'd have been able to hear his scream of pain from the other side of the field. And even somebody who'd never watched football before would know the defender was going to get a red card.

The referee blew his whistle. He pulled out the red card. The defender didn't even complain and neither did his teammates.

"Go on, then," said Seb, pushing me onto the pitch. "See if he's all right."

This was Steve's usual job. He sometimes brought a supermarket bag with a wet sponge in it. He called this the magic sponge and claimed it could help with most injuries, although it never did.

Jacob lay on his back and held his leg; his face was contorted with pain. I could see blood coming through his sock.

"Are you OK?" I asked.

"No," he replied.

I didn't really know what to do.

"Where's Steve?" asked Jacob's mum, striding over. "This is an absolute joke!" she told the referee. Next, she turned to shout at John Whitgift. "You ought to be ashamed of your team!"

She bent over and helped Jacob to his feet.

"It hurts, Mum," he said.

"I bet it does. You've opened up that cut you got when you ran into the coffee table chasing your brother. There'll be no more football for you today. At least your face is OK."

It took a second for the realisation to hit.

"Sorry, Alfie," he said, as he was half-helped, half-carried off by his mum.

Because he knew what it meant. It meant that I'd have to play.

# 9 Goals win games

It happened in a blur. I stood on the halfway line, imagining that if I copied what Jacob might do, I could get away without embarrassing myself. Because that, now, was what I was mainly worried about. Well, also Steve's reaction when he escaped from the toilet.

Steel City had a goal kick, after Tara had launched the ball upfield from her penalty spot with so much pace I had no chance of ever catching it, and it went out of play. Their keeper took the resulting goal kick, and I don't know what they were thinking. There was no wind or anything, it was probably a mis-hit, but the ball ballooned far up in the sky and at a really sharp angle.

I could see that it wasn't going to cross into our half, so I started to jog, which was exactly what Jacob might have done. One defender followed me, while the others kept watch on the edge of their box. And, until the very last second, they'd nothing to worry about whatsoever.

Now, if I had any skill, I might have controlled the ball, because I'd judged exactly where it was going to land, just on the edge of penalty box. But unfortunately, I don't. The ball struck the very top of my head and knocked me to the ground.

The opposition players laughed, and I heard Seb call from the touchline, asking if I was hurt. Mum shouted: "Get yourself up, lad."

But then, two of the strangest things happened:

1. The laughter stopped.

2. There was lots of cheering.

I lifted my head from the grass. And I could hardly believe what I saw. The Steel City Star goalkeeper was sprawled in the back of their goal and the ball was happily nestled in the corner of the net. The defenders had their hands on their hips and stared at the ground. Somehow, accidentally, and you're not going to believe it but: I'd scored a goal.

Before I could fully compute what was happening, I was crushed by the combined weight of my team jumping onto me. I managed to crawl out of the scrum; I'd never seen everyone look so happy.

"What happened?" I asked, as Chris hugged me.

"It hit your head, looped over the defence, their goalkeeper slipped, and the ball, like, dribbled in."

Steel City Stars kicked off. They managed maybe two passes before the final whistle blew. I've never known our families scream and yell with so much excitement. And, as the team ran to mob me once again, I caught sight of John Whitgift pulling off his sunglasses and throwing them to the ground, his orange face contorted into a snarl.

Our celebrations were cut short by a voice. "Would someone kindly tell me what's going on? First, some joker locks me in the toilet; next, you lot are dancing a merry jig in the centre circle."

There was a moment of awkward silence, until …

"We won, gaffer," said Bish, in a tiny voice.

"Alfie scored!' said Dylan. "What a legend."

"We're in the final!" added Tara. "I legit can't believe it."

Conscious of the approaching parents, you could see Steve deciding it was best to play along.

"What did I tell you? Good job. It was all that running about that won it for us," he said, from clenched teeth. "You did it for your coach, locked in a toilet, good job, I'm proud of you."

And, for the very first time ever, my team lifted me onto their shoulders and they cheered and they bounced me and I felt a bit sick to be honest. I was relieved when Mum told them to put me down because she couldn't be doing with any broken bones.

FPO

# 10 He almost hit it too well

Hillsborough's an amazing old stadium. In the 1930s, 72,000 fans fitted in there to watch a quarter-final against Manchester City. It holds about half that number now but, on the day of our cup final, there might have been about 100 watching.

It didn't matter. Two weeks after the semi-final, I sat on the home bench, alongside Sonny. He was the coach of the U12s who we borrowed for the day; he was happy to step in *and* take on board *any* tactical suggestions.

Having told the club that he was leaving for Steel City, the decision was made to drop Steve for our final game, ex-pro or not. None of us were too sad about this.

The dugout had very comfy seats, and I enjoyed every second of sitting there. I even came on for the last five minutes because Seb's legs continued to be different lengths, apparently, and he couldn't run for long.

We played a team from the north of the city, Walkley FC. Jacob was fit for the final and I'd love to tell you he scored a last-minute winner. But football, as any fan will tell you, doesn't always have a fairytale ending. Man City keep winning the Premier League, for instance.

We lost 4-0.

But, still, I'll always have the memory of the semi-final, my coaching of the team, and my last-minute winner. Even if it was an accident. That and my runners-up medal too.

Steve never found out who locked him in the toilet. He officially left the team shortly after our final defeat to join the Steel City Stars. We struggled to find a replacement until Mum volunteered. She said she'd heard nothing from me other than tactics for months and months, so she felt like she'd completed her coaching badges.

I never thought it possible that a manager would have us running more than Steve. But I'd never before been in a football team coached by my mother.

Still, it's all good. I've been managing Sheffield Wednesday for 20 seasons now on Football Manager, I've won every trophy multiple times and even turned down the England job. Too much stress. As if we're ever going to win the World Cup without a decent defence.

One Saturday afternoon, I even rang 606 again. Once more, Dad, Mum and Sammy sat around the kitchen table.

"And now we have Alfie from Sheffield, who's a repeat caller, I hear. How's it going, Alfie? Are you here to talk United?" asked Ricky Stone.

"Never," I said. "I'm a Wednesday fan."

"So what do you want to say?"

"Just that I sometimes wonder why the smaller teams don't use the long ball more often. It's a decent way of beating a high press."

The two pundits chuckled.

"Oh, right," said Matt Weston. "I remember you from the last time. What did I say back then?"

"That if I played football as well as I talked it, I'd be a superstar," I replied.

"Well ... do you have a team, Alfie?" asked Ricky Stone. "I don't think you ever said."

"I do," I replied. "And I coached them to the final of the U11 Sheffield Youth Cup. *And* I scored the winner in the last-minute of the semi-final."

This time, Sammy wasn't kicking me. He was grinning and nodding.

I've come to terms with not being the most technically gifted footballer, because I reckon there may still be some future in coaching for me. I just need to persuade Mum to do a bit more ball work in training first.

# Sheffield Gazette

Suprise success for Fulwood Rangers in semi-final

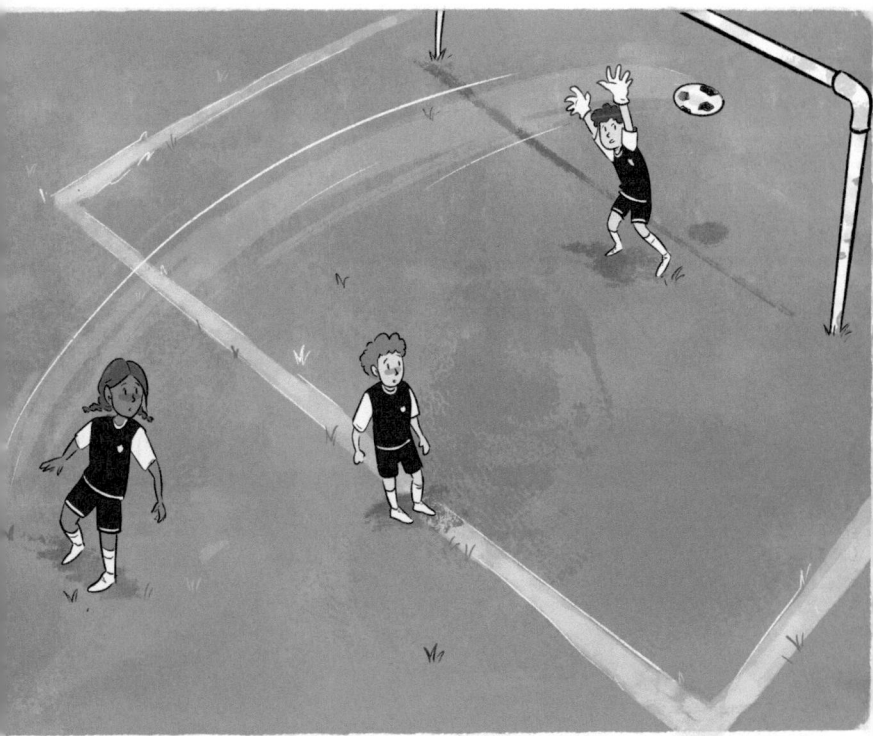

# Book Club Questions

Why do you think Alfie is so reluctant to manage the team at first?

Have you been part of a sports team? What did you enjoy about it?

Why do you think the kids in the team rebel during halftime?

What is the most important lesson Alfie learns by the end of the story?

If you were a player on Alfie's team, what role do you think you would play?

What makes Alfie a unique character compared to other coaches in sports stories?

How does Alfie's relationship with the team evolve throughout the book?

Why do you think it's important to do things that you enjoy, not just because you're good at them?

Do you think the book conveys a message about teamwork and perseverance?

What do you think will happen to Alfie and his team next?

# About the author

**Do you support a football team?**
Sheffield Wednesday!

**Why do you like writing about sports?**
Someone clever once said that everything they'd learnt in philosophy could be found in a football match. Drama! Comedy! Tension! Disappointment! Get past the 0-0 draws and what's not to like?

*Tom Mitchell*

**Who is your favourite character in the book and why?**
Whisper it quietly but I quite like Steve. As a father to two football-mad kids, I admire his attitude to coaching children!

**Which is your favourite illustration in the book?**
They're all great but Steve in his foldable chair, cup of tea in hand, as the kids jog past is very funny.

**What do you most want readers to take away from reading this book?**
It's okay to do stuff because you enjoy it. Life doesn't have to be a competition.

**What was your favourite book as a child?**
I really liked a book called The Box of Delights.
A young boy needs to protect a magical box from
a gang of villains. But that description doesn't
do it justice. The story is wild and dreamlike and
reminds me of Christmas.

**How did you come up with the character of
Steve?**
It's always struck me that it must be a strange
existence, being a retired professional footballer.
Being better at football than everyone you know,
getting paid to play a game and then, in your mid-
thirties, having to stop. Steve was my attempt to
imagine what that must be like.

**Have you ever played in a sports team?**
Umm ... a long time ago and not very successfully.
But my sons will tell you that this doesn't stop me
describing, in detail, every one of the handful of
goals I scored back then.

**Collins**
**BIG CAT**

Published by Collins
An imprint of HarperCollins*Publishers*

The News Building
1 London Bridge Street
London SE1 9GF
UK

1st Floor, Watermarque
Building
Ringsend Road
Dublin 4
Ireland

10 9 8 7 6 5 4 3 2 1

ISBN 978-0-00-874475-5

British Library Cataloguing-in-Publication Data
A catalogue record for this publication is available from the British Library.

Author: Tom Mitchell
Illustrator: Amy Lane (Beehive Illustration)
Publisher: Laura White
Commissioning editor: Holly Woolnough
Development editor: Zoë Clarke
Product manager: Holly Woolnough
Content editor: Selin Akca
Copyeditor: Sally Byford
Proofreader: Catherine Dakin
Reviewer: Lisa Davis
Cover designer: Sarah Finan
Internal design: 2Hoots Publishing Services Ltd
Typesetter: Jouve India Ltd
Production controller: Katharine Willard

Collins would like to thank the teachers and children at Grange Primary School, Southwark, for being part of the development of Big Cat Read On.

Printed in the UK.

**MIX**
Paper | Supporting
responsible forestry
**FSC**
www.fsc.org
**FSC™ C007454**

Get the latest Collins Big Cat news at
collins.co.uk/collinsbigcat